TREE MUSKETEERS

D0973549

OTHER NOVELS BY NORMA CHARLES

Runner (Red Deer Press, 2017)

Last Chance Island (Ronsdale, 2016)

Run Marco, Run (Ronsdale, 2011)

Chasing a Star (Ronsdale, 2009)

Bank Job (Orca, 2009, with James Heneghan)

The Girl in the Backseat (Ronsdale, 2008)

Boxcar Kid (Dundurn, 2007)

Sophie's Friend in Need (Beach Holme, 2004)

All the Way to Mexico (Raincoast, 2003)

Fuzzy Wuzzy (Coteau, 2002)

Criss Cross, Double Cross (Beach Holme, 2002)

The Accomplice (Raincoast, 2001)

Sophie, Sea to Sea (Beach Holme, 1999)

Runaway (Coteau, 1999)

Dolphin Alert! (Nelson, 1998)

Darlene's Shadow (General, 1991)

A bientôt, Croco (Scholastic, 1991)

See You Later, Alligator (Scholastic, 1991)

April Fool Heroes (Nelson, 1989)

Un poney embarrassant (Les Editions Héritage, 1989)

No Place for a Horse (General, 1988)

Amanda Grows Up (Scholastic, 1978)

Tree
Musketeers

Norma Charles

RONSDALE PRESS

TREE MUSKETEERS

RONSDALE PRESS
3350 West 21st Avenue, Vancouver, B.C., Canada V6S 1G7
www.ronsdalepress.com

Typesetting: Julie Cochrane, in Minion 12 pt on 16
Cover Art: Kathryn Shoemaker
Illustrations: Kathryn Shoemaker
Paper: 70 lb. Husky Offset White (FSC) 100% post-consumer waste,
    totally chlorine-free and acid-free

Ronsdale Press wishes to thank the following for their support of its publishing program: the Canada Council for the Arts, the Government of Canada, the British Columbia Arts Council, and the Province of British Columbia through the British Columbia Book Publishing Tax Credit program.

Library and Archives Canada Cataloguing in Publication

Charles, Norma M., author
    Tree musketeers / Norma Charles; illustrations by Kathryn Shoemaker.

Issued in print and electronic formats.
ISBN 978-1-55380-550-2 (softcover)
ISBN 978-1-55380-551-9 (ebook) / ISBN 978-1-55380-552-6 (pdf)

    I. Shoemaker, Kathryn E., illustrator   II. Title.

PS8555.H4224T74 2018   jC813'.54   C2018-904077-7   C2018-904078-5

At Ronsdale Press we are committed to protecting the environment. To this end we are working with Canopy and printers to phase out our use of paper produced from ancient forests. This book is one step towards that goal.

Printed in Canada by Island Blue, Victoria, B.C.

for sweet Coco

ACKNOWLEDGEMENTS

Thanks, as always, to my family, for inspiring
this book, for your patience in hearing the story
time and time again, and for your continuing
encouragement and support.

Chapter 1

"BOYS AND GIRLS. Listen up," my new teacher Mr. Grady says. "This is Jeanie Leclare. She has just arrived with her family from Saskatchewan. I'm sure everyone will make her welcome."

All the kids in the class look up from their books and stare at me while Mr. Grady points to a vacant desk beside the windows. When I sit down, I notice it's behind a girl with red hair tied back in a loose ponytail.

She turns around and sort-of smiles and nods a welcome. My churning stomach eases a bit. At least there's *one* friendly face in here.

But I *so* miss my old friends. I don't want to be here. Vancouver feels like a million miles away from my old school. It sure is tough being the new kid in December, halfway through the year, in a new town. A new province, even.

Here in my new grade five class, it's silent reading period. Everyone's reading. The teacher, as well. There's not much choice left on the silent reading shelf at the back of the classroom. Not a single book about cats. So I choose the next best thing. A book about a dog. *A Great Dane Called Big Morgan.*

Before opening the book, I check the view out the window beside my desk. At the edge of the school grounds, there's an evergreen tree with waving branches. It's enormous. Probably the biggest tree I've ever seen. Behind it is a cute Hansel and Gretel gingerbread kind-of house.

A truck with an orange excavator on a flatbed trailer is stopping in front of the little house. Two men get out to unload the excavator. Another man with his arms crossed watches them. He's big and burly. He looks familiar. My insides jolt as I recognize him. My Uncle Berny!

I haven't seen him since the summer when he came to visit us in Sandberg. But I'm sure it's him. After a few minutes, he drives off in a white van.

I watch as the two other men staple a fence of red plastic tape around the yard. Danger.

One man climbs into the orange excavator. It rumbles toward the house. Its motor grinds and its shovel jaws gape open hungrily.

The big machine confronts the little house, shovel snapping. Goliath and David.

I stiffen.

The shovel wallops the house! The house shudders, its glass windows splintering.

The shovel wallops it again. And again.

Crash! One side of the house crumples.

Everyone in class gasps. Including me.

We all rush over to crowd around the window ledge. Even the teacher.

The monster shovel bashes the little house again. And again. Until the house topples over and completely collapses in on itself. The roof, the walls crash into a cloud of debris.

All that's left is the brick chimney. It's like the last brave soldier left standing after a mighty battle.

The kids squeal.

Now the mighty shovel attacks that brick chimney. Bash! Smack!

I can't watch. I have to look away.

"Holy moly!" a boy with curly black hair says. "See that baby shake, rattle and roll!"

"Hoo-ie!" a girl shouts. "Another one hits the dust!"

"No," another kid says. "How can they do that?"

"Oh, it was such a sweet little house," moans the redhead who sits in front of me.

I guess she won't be my friend after all. Not when she

finds out it's my uncle's construction company that just destroyed that cute house.

"Fun's over now, boys and girls." Mr. Grady claps his hands. "Sit down, everyone. Let's get back to our reading."

I peel myself from the window ledge and return to my seat where I pick up my novel. I keep seeing the little house cringe and shudder and finally collapse under the giant shovel. When everyone finds out about my uncle's company, they'll all hate me, for sure.

My nose is running but I don't have a tissue, so I have to wipe it on the back of my hand. My eyes sting. I sniff, blink hard and stare down at my book but the letters wobble. I can't read a word.

By the time recess bell rings, the *entire* little house has vanished. Squashed to nothing under the heavy excavator. All that's left are piles of rubble and a small wooden tool shed at the corner of the lot. And it's all my uncle's fault.

Then something even *more* terrible happens.

The excavator starts rumbling toward the side of the yard.

It's heading straight for the giant evergreen tree!

I slip back to the window to watch.

"No, no." I grip the window ledge. "Not the tree! They can't knock down that beautiful tree."

"Aren't you coming for recess?" the redhead asks me.

"Look! That excavator. It's heading for the tree."

"No. Not *our* tree!" she shouts. "We've got to stop it!"

I follow her and so do a couple other girls. We grab our jackets and dash down the hall and out a side door. We shoot across the school grounds and duck under the red danger tape fence.

"Stop!" We're shouting and waving our arms at the excavator like a bunch of mad traffic controllers. "Stop! Stop!"

But the excavator keeps on chugging right at us.

Does the operator even see us?

"Stop!" we yell again. "Stop! Stop!"

I yell so loud, my throat hurts. But the excavator thumps even louder as it grinds closer and closer, its giant shovel snapping greedily.

The excavator's not stopping. I hold my breath.

"Hey, kids." A man sticks his head out of the cab. "Get out of the way! You'll get hurt."

"We're not moving!" the redhead yells at him in her very loud voice. She shakes both fists. "You *can't* knock down this tree. It's ours!"

"What? Can't hear you." The man turns off the motor and climbs out of the cab. "Now what's going on here? I told you kids to move. We've got to clear away those bushes. It's dangerous around here. You're going to get hurt."

By now, a bunch of other kids has scrambled over the piles of debris to join us. My heart's pounding.

"This tree! You *can't* knock it down!" the girl repeats. "There . . . there's a woodpecker's nest up there."

"That's right!" one of the other kids shouts, waving his arms.

"What? A woodpecker's nest?" The man grins. "Come on, kids. I've got work to do. I have to clear away those bushes. You're in my way. You shouldn't be here. Like I said, it's dangerous."

"But . . . but my uncle's Berny Leclare," I pipe up in my loudest voice. It sounds like a tin whistle beside the redhead's trumpet. "I'm *sure* he wouldn't want this tree damaged."

"So your uncle's Berny Leclare, the contractor in charge, eh?" The man scratches his head and checks his watch. "We'll see what he says. We've got to leave now, for another job down on 32nd. But we'll be coming back tomorrow or the next day. With chainsaws. And the tree removal crew."

He climbs back into the cab and guides the excavator back to the flatbed trailer. They load up and drive away.

The redhead turns to me. "Is your uncle *really* the guy whose company wrecked that cute house?"

I shrug.

"Berny S. Leclare, contractor?" She points to the APPLICATION FOR DEVELOPMENT sign in front of the property. "That's *your* uncle?" Her eyes are huge. It's like she can't believe anything so horrible is even possible.

I shrug again.

"So your uncle is one of those awful . . . *developers*?" She screws up her nose like her mouth's full of nasty medicine. "Developers who knock down nice old homes and build those ugly monster houses?"

"Well, um, actually, yes." I have to admit it. "He is my uncle."

"Well, in my opinion, your uncle's a total jerk. How could he ever do such a terrible thing?"

I turn away and kick a rock so hard it rolls past the danger tape fence onto the pile of rubble. My lips feel like tight rubber bands.

"You heard what that guy said?" The girl bounces in front of me and yells in my face. "Tree removal crew! With chainsaws! Like, *tomorrow!*"

I force my rubber-band lips to move. "I'll talk to my uncle. Tonight. Okay?"

I cross my fingers for good luck. Except for this morning, I haven't even seen my uncle since we moved to this awful city.

The bell ends recess and pulls us all back to class.

Chapter 2

AFTER RECESS, MR. GRADY announces it's gym period, so the class lines up at the classroom door. He's wearing a dark blue sweater with silvery buttons down the front. As he waits impatiently for us, his thick eyebrows are like two caterpillars playing follow-the-leader across his forehead. He's got the kind of face that doesn't look used to smiling. It's long with downward creases at the sides of his mouth.

I stare at him and yearn for jolly Mrs. Fan who was my teacher at my old school in Sandberg. No one else seems concerned about gym strip, so I don't worry about it either.

As we follow Mr. Grady along the hall to the gym, two

by two, I try to be the redhead's partner. But she pulls forward to walk beside another girl. I know she's mad at me because of my uncle. The other kids avoid me like I've got rabies. So I end up walking down to the gym alone.

When we get there, Mr. Grady divides us into four groups. We practise whacking volleyballs over the volleyball nets.

"No, Jeanie!" he yells at me. "Hit the ball with the heel of your palm, like this." He demonstrates.

Everyone stares while I blush and try again. My palm stings, but not as much as when I hit the ball with my whole hand.

After a few minutes, Mr. Grady says, "Okay, class. We've got time for a quick game. Let's get you into teams."

I follow the other kids and sit on one of the low wooden benches at the edge of the gym.

"Team captains for today will be Trudy and Mojo," he says. "Remember, this is co-ed. We want mixed boys *and* girls teams."

Trudy's a blonde girl even shorter than me. Her first pick is the girl with red hair. I find out her name is Isabelle. Mojo chooses his buddy, George.

"Remember, guys. Mixed teams," Mr. Grady reminds them.

I sit tall. I hate being the last one chosen. Isabelle whispers to Trudy. Then Trudy picks Robert, a lanky boy with big feet.

Isabelle probably told her not to pick me. They wouldn't

want someone from a family of house demolishers and tree killers on their team.

A few other kids are chosen. My hands are sweating. I *can't* be last! I sit up even taller.

Mojo calls out, "Jeanie."

Oh well. Better to be picked by Mojo than be loser-last.

After the teams are all chosen, we start playing. There are about fifteen players on each side of the net, which makes it crowded. That's okay. I head for the back row of my team where I can hide out.

During the game, I can't stop thinking about the evergreen tree. Why destroy it just to build another stupid house? There are already thousands of houses crowding this city. But there aren't many trees as big as that giant evergreen.

Also, Isabelle and the other kids seem to be bent on saving the tree. If I want any friends at this new school, I'll have to make darn sure nothing happens to it. They'll all hate me *forever* if my family destroys something so important.

But what can I do about it?

In the game, I manage to stick to the back row so I don't have to hit the ball. But while I'm standing there thinking about the tree and all, the ball shoots right at my legs. Hard. I trip over it and fall flat on my stomach. Splat. And bash my chin on the floor. For a second, I actually see stars. When my vision clears, Mojo's there.

"You okay?" He looks concerned.

"I'm fine," I mutter, shaking my head, getting back up.

The other team, including Isabelle and Trudy, hoots with laughter. My cheeks burn with embarrassment. Talk about a loser.

A few minutes later, Mr. Grady blows his whistle. "All right, class. Time to pack it up."

Chapter 3

THE REST OF THE morning drags through social studies. The class is studying Australia, so it's all kangaroos and koalas and wombats. Finally, the lunch bell rings.

I hang around getting my lunch bag and parka from the hooks at the back of the classroom. I'm not sure where to go to eat.

Mr. Grady comes over. "Isabelle. Show our new friend where the lunchroom is, will you?"

Isabelle screws up her nose, and he raises his thick eyebrows at her. So she shrugs and looks at me with a fake smile. "Want to have lunch with us, Jeanie?"

"Sure," I mutter, although I know she doesn't want me along. It's probably better to hang out with your Enemy

Number One than be alone in a sea of strangers.

I follow her and two other girls along the hall filled with clamouring kids. We go down some side stairs to the lunchroom in the basement. Noise echoes off the cement walls. We push past the little kids who are all gabbing away, shoving food into their mouths. We get to a long table filled mainly with other girls who look like they're in grade five like us.

It's cold down here in the basement. So when Isabelle sits on the long bench, she pulls her purple rain jacket over her shoulders. The other two girls huddle under their rain jackets as well.

I'm freezing, but I can't put on my parka. It's so thick and lumpy it makes me look like a stuffed teddy bear. So I sit on it and pull my shirt sleeves down over my elbows. Every time the door opens, a draft blows up my back and I think of Siberia.

If only I had a cool rain jacket like Isabelle's and her friends' instead of this babyish teddy-bear parka . . .

"Auditions for the winter musical after school. You guys going?" one of the girls asks Isabelle. It's Trudy, the short blonde girl who was team captain in gym.

"Sure thing!" Isabelle says as she dumps her lunch onto the table. A pack of Lunch Munch crackers and cheese, chocolate chip cookies and a banana with a blue Chiquita sticker. Even her lunch is cool.

She sticks the banana sticker on her nose. "Dah, da-da-

da. Dah! Presenting *Santa Lost in Mish-Mash Land*," she announces in her booming voice.

The other girls laugh so I do too. Maybe a bit too loudly.

"Mr. G.'s musical's going to be so sweet!" Isabelle says, blowing off the sticker. "Everything he does in music is sweet. Sometimes I think it's the only thing he truly cares about. That and reading us novels. What about you, Jeanie? Are you trying out for the musical?"

Now she's being nice to me? Is it just because she likes an audience?

"What's it about?" I nibble my sandwich. Peanut butter. Sticks to the roof of my mouth. Makes my tongue feel as dry as sandpaper.

"It's a musical we're putting on before the holidays. We've already learned all the songs in music class. Some pretty good rap stuff, like 'Merry Monsters' Hand Jive' and 'Surfin' Santa.' It's the best. Goes like: Surfin' Santa, Surfin' Santa, Surfin' Santa, Santa Claus." She sings loudly, sort of through her nose.

Kids stop eating to stare at her. She grins at them. She sure doesn't mind all the attention.

Trudy nods at me. "Best thing about being in the musical is you get time off school to practise." She takes a sip of apple juice from a juice box. "So you've got to try out for it. Everyone does."

"But I can't dance or sing or anything," I say. I'm trying to peel the peanut butter from the roof of my mouth with my sandpaper tongue. Wish I'd brought a juice box like Trudy's.

It's not strictly true that I totally *can't* sing. I was Wendy in our musical last spring when we did *Peter Pan* at my old school in Sandberg and it was quite a big singing part.

"Try out for the chorus then," Trudy tells me. "Anyone can get into that. Just jump around the·stage and sing along with everyone else. That's what I'm doing."

"I've *got* to get the part of Mr. Biggy-Big-Ears!" Isabelle says. "If I don't, I'll probably end up being Boo-boo Peep or something equally stupid. And be forced to wear one of those cutesy dresses like last year when I had to be a fairy princess. Talk about embarrassing!"

"Okay, I'll go." I dump crackers from my bag. "But who's Mr. Biggy-Big-Ears?"

"You haven't heard of Mr. Biggy-Big-Ears?"

I shrug and shake my head.

Isabelle stares at me like I'm as dumb as a bowl of bananas.

Trudy comes to my rescue. "Mr. Biggy-Big-Ears is a sort-of monster who has these really huge ears." She puts her hands at the sides of her face and waves. "Everyone always makes fun of him, but he finishes up being the hero of the story because at the end, he saves Santa."

"You should say, '*she* saves Santa,' because it's going to be *Ms.* Biggy-Big-Ears when *I* get the part," Isabelle tells her.

Talk about confidence!

"Okay, *she's* going to be the hero." Trudy nods.

"Anyways," Isabelle says. "If you guys come to the try-outs after school and clap *really* loud after my song, the teachers will think I'm just so terrific."

"No prob. We'll hoot and cheer for you too," the other girl says in a quiet voice. Her name's Mee-Sue. She's a tall Asian girl with long shiny black hair and straight bangs that cover her eyebrows.

I just nod because the crackers have made my mouth even drier. I look around for a water fountain but don't see one. I try swallowing again and almost gag.

The other girls get up to leave. I pick up my parka and follow them outside like a timid mouse trailing a band of cats pretending to be nice.

It's raining, so we spend the rest of lunch hour hanging out under a covered area attached to the main school building. The girls practise singing the songs from the musical. They're right that the songs are really catchy. They mostly ignore me, but it's good not to have to spend the whole rest of noon hour standing around alone.

After school, Mr. Grady reminds the class about the musical auditions. "But before you leave, hand in your math exercise books, please."

"But I'm not finished," a boy in a back seat says.

"Who else hasn't finished their math?" The teacher looks around the class.

Yikes! I have to raise my hand. So do three other kids. All boys.

The teacher frowns at us. "It must be done before you go home so I can mark it tonight. You can leave your books on my desk when you're finished."

"See you later in the gym," Isabelle whispers as she leaves. "Don't forget to clap really loud."

"Right." I flip open the math book.

After the teacher's gone, the boys fool around. But I ignore them and rush through the last six math questions. When they're done, I drop my exercise book on Mr. Grady's desk, then scoot downstairs to the gym for the auditions.

Chapter 4

ISABELLE'S UP ON stage, singing away when I arrive. The stage is at one end of the big drafty gym, where about fifty kids and a couple of teachers sit on low benches watching Isabelle perform.

She's belting out "Sing a Song of Sixpence" in her loud nasal voice while Mr. Grady bangs out the tune on the piano.

I slouch down onto a bench. Isabelle sure is brave to sing like that, in front of all these people.

"And pecked off her nose!" She finishes and bows.

When Isabelle hits that last note off-key, Mr. G.'s eyebrows flinch. But I clap and hoot with the rest of the kids. I even stamp my feet as loud as I can.

Isabelle notices because when she heads to her seat, she grins in my direction.

I smile back and give her a thumbs-up.

"Thank you, Isabelle," the teacher says. "Now we'll hear from Megan . . ."

After a while, it's time for what I've come for. Tryouts for the chorus.

"All right. If you want to be in the chorus, come up on stage," Mr. Grady says.

I follow a bunch of other kids and we line up in a row on the stage. The kids all turn to face the big gym and the audience, so I turn too.

I'm standing at the end of the line next to Mee-Sue, and my heart is thumping in my chest. It feels so high up here on the stage. Conspicuous. I take a deep breath and tell myself to be calm.

Why am I doing this? I ask myself.

"Right," Mr. Grady says. "When it's your turn, I want each of you to take a step forward and sing the first thing that comes into your head. Starting . . ." And he points to me!

I just about faint.

He nods and stands there with his arms crossed, staring at me, waiting.

Everyone is waiting.

I step forward and clear my throat, telling myself, *All right. Big breath. Stand up straight and tall.* Like Mrs. Fan, the teacher at my old school, always told us.

I open my mouth and the first thing that comes out is, "When you wish upon a star, makes no difference who . . ." What a dorky song. Why did I ever choose that one?

But soon Mr. Grady says, "Thank you, Jeanie. Good job." And he jots some notes onto his clipboard. "Next. Mee-Sue . . ."

Mee-Sue's singing voice is even quieter than her talking voice. "How much is that doggie . . ."

"Good. Thanks, Mee-Sue." Mr. Grady nods and jots and listens to each of the other kids while we're all standing up there. It feels like *hours* but is probably only a few minutes. Finally, he comes to the last kid in the row. It's Trudy and her singing voice is even quieter than Mee-Sue's, which is a surprise because I've heard her talking loud enough.

"Looks like that's all the time we have for auditions today." Mr. Grady glances at his watch. "But if you want to be in the chorus, I think we can use you all. Just sign up on this clipboard on your way out."

Hey. That means we all made it. I turn and grin at Mee-Sue, and she grins back.

Mr. Grady picks up another clipboard from the top of his piano. "We'll meet here every morning at eight o'clock until the day of the concert. So don't sign up unless you can commit to that. Meanwhile, the leads so far are: Santa: Mojo Desantos."

"Right on!" Mojo jumps up and bows to everyone.

"And Mr. Biggy-Big-Ears will be . . ." The teacher scans

his notes. Everyone's holding their breath. "Maybe we'll change that to *Ms.* Biggy-Big-Ears . . . Isabelle Seconi."

Isabelle squeals and smacks hands with the girls beside her.

* * *

After signing up for the chorus with Mee-Sue and Trudy, I follow Isabelle outside. It's still raining and already so dark, the street lights in front of the school are on.

I zip up my puffy teddy-bear parka and push my hands deep into the pockets. The rain's icy on my face and my parka soaks up the drops like a sponge. Again, I wish for a trendy rain jacket like Isabelle's.

"Thanks for clapping and stamping your feet," Isabelle says when I catch up to her. She pulls her hood over her red hair. "I'm sure that's why I got the Ms. Biggy-Big-Ears part."

"They would have chosen you anyway. You're a good singer."

Well, loud anyway, I think to myself. *Loud as a farmer's old combine working full blast in a wheat field.*

"About our tree. Want to see why it's so special?"

"All right. I guess." I follow her to the big evergreen at the edge of the school grounds.

"For one thing, we built a cool fort in it," Isabelle says. "Want to check it out?"

"Okay."

"Right this way." Isabelle ducks under the tree. She catches the lowest branch and swings up into the tree.

"You mean we can't see your fort from down here?" I call up to her. I'm not used to climbing trees. In fact, I can't remember when I've *ever* climbed one. There weren't many tall trees in Sandberg, Saskatchewan.

"Course not," she yells at me from above.

"All right. Here goes." I have to jump my hardest to reach the same branch. As I swing my leg over it, my face is showered with icy raindrops. Blinking hard, I manage to pull myself into a sitting position. I grab another branch above my head and cautiously stand. The branches sway like a team of restless horses. It's like they're trying to buck me off, so I have to hold on tighter.

Then I shuffle along the branch to the broad trunk where the branches are thicker and steadier. That feels better. But then I make the mistake of glancing down and see how high I am.

"Yikes!" I squeeze my eyes shut and clutch the branches even tighter.

"So are you coming up or what?" Isabelle yells down at me from her higher perch.

"I'm coming. I'm coming." Hugging the trunk, I slowly follow Isabelle upward. Bits of tree debris fly into my eyes. Now I can't see anything. I have to stop and rub my eyes. I don't think I'm cut out for this tree-climbing stuff.

The fort turns out to be just a few planks stretched

across some branches to make a slanting floor, and there's one wobbly side. I don't think it's really much of a fort, but I don't say.

"We started building it last summer," Isabelle tells me. "We even had a pretty good roof, but it got wrecked in a storm last month and we haven't had time to fix it. Besides, we need more lumber and nails and stuff."

"Maybe I could try and get some boards from my dad."

"Great!" Isabelle's smile flashes at me in the dim light. "Then you could be part of our club."

"What club?"

"Trudy, Mee-Sue and a couple other girls. We call it the Tree Climbers Club."

"Cool."

"We're building this fort for our clubhouse. But we can't do much in the winter. The club's mostly in the summer when it doesn't get dark so early, you know?"

"A roof would be good for when it rains. Does it always rain so much in Vancouver? It hasn't stopped for five minutes since we got here last week."

Isabelle shrugs. "You get used to it. My mom says rain's better than shovelling snow."

"But snow's *so* fun. We have this great skating rink back home in Sandberg on a pond out behind the school. Practically every day after school all winter, me and my friends, we met there with our skates and . . ."

"So where's this Sandberg?"

"In Saskatchewan. South of Regina, you know?"

Isabelle shrugs again, obviously bored. "Hey, want to see something really cool?"

"Sure."

"Up here." Isabelle slides along the broad branch to the trunk and starts climbing again.

"You mean we have to go even higher?"

"It's not far."

I catch my breath and follow her, still hugging the trunk. We push through the branches higher and higher. It's like climbing one of those pole ladders with steps sticking out all around. But as we climb, the trunk gets narrower. The tree sways in the wind and my stomach pitches.

"Ah, Isabelle, don't you think this is high enough?" My voice squeaks. My legs are trembling and my mouth's even drier than when I was trying to eat my peanut butter sandwich at lunchtime.

"Ever seen a woodpecker's nest up close?"

I can't even open my mouth now. I'm too busy hanging on for dear life.

"It's not that much higher." Isabelle sniffs and wipes her nose on her jacket sleeve. "We climb up here all the time."

I swallow hard. If she knows I'm such a chicken about heights, she won't let me join her Tree Climbers Club. So I take another deep breath and force myself to follow her. The tree is *really* swaying now. I tell myself if Isabelle's not scared, it must be all right. But I don't dare look down. The ground is very, very far below.

Finally she says, "Here it is. In this hole."

I slowly boost myself upward on quaking legs. Clinging to the trunk, I blink until I see a small round hole, the size of my fist. No birds or eggs. Nothing but some dried grass sticking out.

"Pretty cool, eh?" Isabelle says. "It's our secret hiding place for private stuff." She pokes her fingers into the hole. "Nothing's in there now. Woodpeckers come back every spring to raise a family. But we stay away then, when they've got babies."

"Cool," I manage to squeak.

"Now take a look out there. Have you ever seen such a fabulous view?"

I pull in a breath and stare out where she points. Way out beyond the school roof, the city lights sparkle like a blanket of stars. "Wow!"

"When it's really clear, you can see right across the water to the lights on the chairlift going up Grouse Mountain."

An especially strong gust of wind blows by. The tree lurches again and I squeal.

"Not nervous, are you?" Isabelle asks in a flat voice.

"No, no." I hug the tree, my heart pounding. "N-nothing like that."

"Good. Because to belong to the club, you can't be scared of heights. Obviously."

"Course. Obviously." I force the quivering corners of my mouth up into a sort-of smile.

"Guess we can head back down now."

Clinging to the trunk, I feel my way down until finally, I swing from the last branch to the ground. My knees are shaking so hard they crumple under me. I sink down and rub them.

Isabelle lands with a thump beside me. "You okay?"

"Sure. Legs a bit stiff. Not used to climbing. That's all."

"So now do you see why we have to stop them from destroying this tree?"

"It's something special, all right." I notice my watch. "5:02! My mom's going to be so worried!"

"Better get going then."

"Right." Holding onto the tree trunk, I pull myself up. "See you tomorrow."

"Okay. Want to meet here for practice at ten to eight? No later. Mr. G. gets real testy if we're late for practice. And don't forget you said you'd talk to your uncle about saving this tree."

"Right."

I watch Isabelle head for home. Now all I have to do is hope that he'll drop over tonight.

Maybe, just maybe, I've found a new friend?

Now, if only I can get my uncle to say he won't cut down this giant old tree . . .

Chapter 5

OUR NEW HOME is in a basement suite of a big old house about three blocks from school.

I push the gate open and swish through the fallen leaves to the backyard along the path between our house and the neighbour's. I skip down the six steps to the basement door and push it open. Mom's sitting at the table, wiping her eyes with a tissue.

She's not crying, is she? I'm embarrassed, so I almost duck back outside.

But she glances up and smiles a crooked smile. "There you are, sweetie!" She blows her nose.

Mom has dark curly hair and brown eyes like mine.

People say we look alike, but I don't think that's true. She's pretty, but I look, well, ordinary. She usually wears bright, colourful clothes and jingly earrings and always has a friendly smile for everyone.

I shake off my heavy parka. It's sodden with rain. I hang it on the doorknob and peer closer at Mom. Today she's wearing one of Dad's old denim work shirts. And her hair's a mess instead of being tucked into a neat ponytail like it usually is.

"You okay, Mom?"

"Just feeling a little homesick." She sips tea from her favourite blue china cup and dabs her nose again. "Must be getting a cold. Isn't Vancouver's rain something else? It hasn't stopped all day."

"It soaked through my parka." I plop down beside her at the table. My T-shirt clings to my back.

Mom pats my shoulder. "Oh, your shirt's all wet. Better change it before you catch a chill."

I duck into my bedroom off the kitchen and change into a warm fleece hoodie.

When I return to the table, Mom pours me a cup of tea from the big brown pot. "I was getting worried about you, sweetie. It's already dark out there. I was about to go out and start searching for you."

"Sorry, Mom. I stayed after school to try out for a musical my teacher's putting on." I stir some honey into the tea and sip it. Lemon. Makes me start to feel warm all over.

Mom seems to realize her hair is a mess. She tucks it back behind her ears. "So did you make it? Are you going to be in the musical?"

"In the chorus."

"That's great! When's the big production?"

"The Friday before the Christmas holidays."

"Doesn't give you much time to practise."

"I think the kids already know all the music. Mr. Grady's in charge and he's taught everyone the songs in his music classes."

"Getting involved in school activities is the best thing you can do in a new school. Remember how much you loved being in *Peter Pan*?"

I nod. It was fun with all my friends.

"Anyway, next time, please phone if you're going to be late. Vancouver's a big city, you know. We're not in Sandberg any more."

"Don't remind me. In Sandberg, everyone knows everyone. When you were working at Dr. Rosier's office, it was only a block from home so I could check in after school every day."

"Oh, Jeanie. I'm sure we'll both get used to living in the city." Mom sighs and shuts the telephone book she'd been looking through. "Guess I'll get supper started."

"That sure is a thick phone book." I pour myself more tea from Mom's pot. "Were you trying to phone someone?"

"I found the phone book in a drawer in the living room bureau. It's pretty old, but it's got a good Yellow Pages section. I was checking doctors and dentists to see if anyone needs a new receptionist. But nothing yet. Maybe I'll have better luck tomorrow."

"If we'd stayed in Sandberg, you could still be working for Dr. Rosier."

"But you know how your father's always dreamed of having his own construction company. And his brother offering to take him on as a partner is his chance to do exactly that. There just isn't enough work for a self-employed carpenter around Sandberg any more."

"Any chance Uncle Berny will be dropping by tonight?"

"I don't think so. Did you want to see him about something special?"

I shrug. "Maybe I can talk to Dad instead."

* * *

That night, while we're eating a supper of cheeseburgers and tomato soup, I ask Dad if he knows anything about the house next door to the school.

"Small white house with green trim?" he asks, cleaning his glasses on his napkin.

"Used to be. They knocked it down today."

"Good. That means we can get started building the new house soon. It's the first big construction project for your Uncle Berny and me. It's going to be a big family house, four bedrooms and four bathrooms, plus a media room and a two-car garage."

It's all because of my dad's new job with my Uncle Berny's construction company that we had to move to Vancouver when we really belong on the Prairies. All our friends are there, and most of my cousins and aunts and uncles. We had a large comfortable house in Sandberg with a yard for Mom's flower garden, and I had a spacious bedroom with a pullout couch for sleepovers with my friends. But we can't ever move back because my parents had to sell the house.

"You know that big tree that hangs over into the school grounds?" I ask my dad.

"The evergreen? Yes. I've noticed it."

"The kids at school are really worried it'll get chopped down. Everyone just loves that tree."

Dad shrugs. "Don't know what I can do about it."

"The man who was driving the excavator said that it was coming down. But you *can't* chop it down, Dad. You just *can't*. It's way too big and beautiful. The kids all love that tree. Could you talk to Uncle Berny about it?"

"I could try to talk to him. But if the tree's in the way of our new construction, it'll have to come down."

My stomach takes a dive. All the kids at school are *so* going to hate me. Especially Isabelle. I stare at my soup.

"What's the matter, sweetie?" Mom pats my arm. "Not hungry?"

"Guess not," I mumble. "Awfully tired. Maybe I'll just go and read for a while."

I push past the heavy furniture in the murky basement to my bedroom. It's so small I have to shuffle sideways to get between the dresser and the bed. The only thing that's really mine in here is a green frog-shaped cushion Gran made me for my tenth birthday last March. When I hug it, it still smells like my old bedroom in Sandberg, like sweet hay and sage. Way nicer than the damp musty smell of this basement suite.

I glare at the ugly brown bedspread before pulling it over my head.

Chapter 6

THE NEXT MORNING, I wait for Isabelle under the big old evergreen. She comes soon.

"So what happened?" she asks. "Did you talk to your uncle about the tree?"

"No. He didn't come over after all."

"But you *said* you would. You *promised*."

"I asked my dad to talk to him."

"He'd *better*. Or else." Isabelle narrows her eyes and glares at me. Then she sprints off to the gym. I trail behind.

So maybe she's not going to be my friend after all.

In the gym, Mr. Grady outlines the plot for the winter musical. An absent-minded Santa sets out for a jog early one foggy morning with his good friend, Ms. Biggy-Big-

Ears. She's sort of a cross between the Easter Bunny and Bigfoot with these gigantic ears. But Santa gets lost in an unusually thick fog and he ends up in a strange world called Mish-Mash Land.

The Mish-Mash folks, who are mostly monsters of one sort or another, try desperately to help Santa find his way back to the North Pole before Christmas Eve so he can make his deliveries. He's finally led back home by Ms. Biggy-Big-Ears, whose keen hearing detects the excited holiday preparations at the North Pole.

Isabelle doesn't look at me *once* during the whole practice. Man! She sure is mad. Just because I didn't talk to my uncle about the tree.

I try not to care that she's ignoring me and stand beside Trudy on stage with the rest of the chorus, about twenty-five girls and boys. I'm nervous at first, but Trudy knows all the words and actions for the songs, so when we sing along with the main characters, I can follow her. It ends up being pretty easy. I remember Mrs. Fan's instructions about opening your mouth wide and singing out to a spot at the back of the gym.

At one point, I'm standing near the edge of the stage, singing out as loud as I can. Mr. Grady notices me and nods like he's liking what he's hearing.

Then we do "Merry Monsters' Hand Jive." It has such a good beat, my feet start moving on their own. When we finish it, I'm grinning like mad.

I whisper to Trudy, "Hey, this is fun."

She grins back. At least *she's* not mad at me.

The bell rings and ends our practice. It's back to boring classes. Except for reading period. Mr. Grady is reading *The Three Musketeers* to us. He makes the story really exciting by acting out the parts using different voices. He's so dramatic. You can tell his favourite character is the young man, d'Artagnan. He's always getting into trouble trying to save maidens in distress, and the Three Musketeers have to keep rescuing him from being arrested. Then they all clash swords and shout, "All for one and one for all!"

Just when Mr. Grady gets to a really exciting part where the guards are about to capture d'Artagnan and drag him away to prison, he shuts the book. "That's it for today, folks. Time for math."

I groan along with the rest of the class. It's way more fun to listen to Mr. Grady read than do boring old math.

"Plenty to cover today, so let's get down to it, everyone. Take out your math textbooks. Page 67. Review of mixed fractions."

Mixed fractions. I sigh and screw up my nose.

He sees me and frowns. "You'll find a math text in your desk, Jeanie," he tells me.

Everyone gawks at me, the new kid. My heart bounces. So many faces!

I duck behind my desk and take a long time sorting through my textbooks. But I'm really trying to avoid the staring eyes. Eventually I peek out. By then, everyone's lost interest.

I pull out my books and write the questions from the math text into my exercise book. Mega *boring*!

At my old school in Sandberg, we did most of our math at work stations with job cards and fun activities. We cut up pies for fractions and weighed stuff on scales. Math was *fun* there.

Through the window next to my desk, I notice a truck pulling up at the property next door. Two men get out. One of them takes out a measuring tape and starts measuring. It's my dad! I wonder if he's had time to talk to Uncle Berny about the tree. Sure hope so.

"Jeanie." Mr. Grady's voice yanks me back. "Your answer to number 3, please?"

"I . . . um . . . I didn't get that far yet," I mumble.

His caterpillar eyebrows frown. "At this school, we pay attention."

"I got 13½," Trudy says, coming to my rescue.

"Correct, Trudy. Tony, number 4?"

The teacher drones on and on.

Finally the recess bell rings and he dismisses us with a flick of his hand and a "You may go now."

I grab my parka and sprint down the hall and outside, hoping Dad's still there. I dash through the rain and duck under the big evergreen tree. But now, no one's at the building site. Just piles of rain-soaked debris. I missed him. Rats. Now what?

I scan the playground where kids are running around,

chasing soccer balls in the rain. If I try talking to anyone, they'll probably just stare at me and think *tree killer*. Then walk away.

Well, I'm *not* a tree killer. I *love* trees. Especially big beautiful ones like this one.

It's dry here, under the tree's thick branches. And it smells sweet. I lean against the shaggy trunk. It's so huge it'd take at least three kids with their arms outstretched to go around it.

There's nothing even half this big back home in Saskatchewan. Even the tallest poplar trees they planted more than a hundred years ago in front of the cathedral aren't this big.

I walked past those poplars practically every day with my best friend, Josie Fournier. Everyone called us "Double J." Like when we went skating behind the school, kids would yell, "Hey, hey, hey. Here comes Double J."

I wonder if Josie's missing me as much as I'm missing her. Probably not. Bet she's already got a new best friend.

The tree's bark feels almost warm against my shoulders. At least the tree doesn't mind me standing beside it.

A rope dangles from a low branch. I catch it and wrap my legs around the lumpy knot. I swing away from the tree's shelter, out into the rain. Then back under the tree again. Back and forth. Back and forth.

The tree's sweet smell reminds me of my grandmother's cedar chest at the farm. The chest where she keeps extra blankets for when I stay overnight. I hum an old French lullaby my gran used to sing when I was small. "*Fais dodo, Colas, mon p'tit frère . . .*"

As I swing higher, I sort of forget where I am. I sing louder and louder, in time with the swing, until I'm singing full out. "*Fais dodo . . .*"

"Hey! Who's that howling?" Mojo yells from below.

I shut my mouth up tight and think, *Please go away.*

He doesn't.

The boy's friend laughs. "New kid thinks she's a fancy opera star."

Clasping their hands over their hearts and fluttering their eyelids, the two boys wail like a couple of coyotes. "*O sole mio . . .*"

I leap off the rope and dash past them onto the wet playing field. A mucky ball bounces against my legs. A dozen feet pound toward me.

"Hey, kid! Get off the field!" someone yells. "Can't you see we're playing soccer here?"

I've run into the middle of a game! My face flushes hot and prickly. I scuttle off the field, feeling two centimetres tall.

The bell rings, ending recess.

I slink back up to the classroom and into my desk, thinking, *Loser, loser, loser.*

Chapter 7

AFTER RECESS, WE HAVE a free reading period, while at the back of the classroom Mr. Grady rehearses raps from the musical with Mojo.

I flip through my novel, *A Great Dane Called Big Morgan,* and glance out at the evergreen. It waves long fringed branches like a green-fingered giant. It seems be pleading. Begging me to save it from being destroyed and made into firewood or lumber. Or whatever they do when they chop down big trees.

Are kids its last hope?

Just before lunch, a white van with black letters on its side drives up. LECLARE BROTHERS CONSTRUCTION. Uncle Berny!

I nudge Isabelle and whisper, "My uncle's out there."

"Good. We'll talk to him," Isabelle hisses back. "Just hope he doesn't take off before we can get to him."

"Stay there, Uncle Berny," I mutter, staring at the van. "Please don't leave."

But the lunch bell doesn't ring. The classroom's silent now. Even Mojo's back at his desk, flipping through his novel.

Should I ask to go to the washroom then sneak out to talk to Uncle Berny? Maybe not, since his van is in full view of the classroom windows and Mr. Grady would see me.

Hurry and ring, bell! I pray. *Hurry, hurry, hurry.*

Finally, my prayer is answered and the lunch bell rings. But before Mr. Grady dismisses the class, Isabelle and I slam our novels shut and start racing for the door. Isabelle trips over Mojo's foot that's somehow "accidentally" in the aisle.

"Ooof!" she grunts as she crashes down to her knees.

I trip over her, thumping my elbow on a desk. Tears sting my eyes.

"Oops." Mojo hides a grin behind his hand. "Sorry."

"Excuse me, girls. Isabelle and Jeanie." Mr. Grady's deep voice rises above everyone's clatter. "If you don't mind, wait until you're dismissed. Go back and sit down, you two. The rest of you may leave."

While the other kids funnel out of the classroom with their lunch packs, we drag ourselves back to our seats. I hold my sore elbow and my cheeks burn with frustration. We *have* to get out there to catch my uncle before he leaves!

Still grinning, Mojo waves at us as he scampers out the door with George. He can be so annoying. I want to stick out my tongue at him but don't.

"Now, girls." Mr. Grady folds his arms and stares down at us over his glasses. "What's the rush? You have a whole hour for lunch. Surely that's long enough for anyone?"

"Yes, Mr. G." Isabelle ducks, her red hair hiding her face.

Should I explain about my uncle? That we have to catch him before he leaves? No. That would delay us even more. I grit my teeth and nod. I just hope and hope with all my might that when we get outside, he's still there.

The teacher drones on. "Now, girls. This is a prime example of 'haste makes waste.'"

We both nod again like those bobblehead dolls they put on dashboards.

"Now," he says. "I want you to quietly, slowly, carefully, get your lunches and quietly, slowly, carefully, walk out of this classroom. Then quietly, slowly, carefully, walk down to the lunchroom. Is that clear?"

"Yes, Mr. G.," Isabelle says.

"Yes, Mr. Grady," I say.

I follow Isabelle as we quietly, slowly, carefully get our lunches.

We quietly, slowly, carefully walk to the classroom door.

We quietly, slowly, carefully go out the door.

Then we race down the hall, gallop down the steps, crash open the outside door, and shoot across the school-yard . . .

. . . Just as Uncle Berny's van pulls away.

"Uncle Berny!" I yell, waving my arms like a maniac. "Uncle Berny!"

Isabelle is panting right behind me.

Oh no! We've missed him. I wave harder.

The van turns the corner. Then it screeches to a stop. It backs up and Uncle Berny opens the door. He's as big and burly as ever, wearing dusty jeans and a plaid work shirt with a black padded vest.

"Jeanie! I thought that was you." A wide grin creases his face. "So how do you like living in the big city?"

"Oh, Uncle Berny!" I skid to a stop. Isabelle crashes into my back.

"Easy now." My uncle catches me before I fall over. "So what's happening, kiddo? I got a call from one of my men and he says there's some kind of problem here . . ."

"It's the tree, Uncle!" I gasp, trying to catch my breath. "You *can't* cut it down. You just *can't!*"

"The tree?" His brow wrinkles and he looks where I point.

"You can't let anything happen to *our* cedar tree!" Isabelle pipes up.

"Why not? What's so special about it? It's just a tree."

"There ... there's a nest up there," she tells him. "A woodpecker's nest!"

I pull in a deep breath. "Besides, all the kids climb it. They built a tree fort. And they have a rope swing. It's sort

of like the main thing to play with around here. And . . . and it's a beautiful old tree, Uncle Berny. You can't just go and cut it down. Think about the *environment!*"

"Well . . ." he says, scratching his head. "I guess I could talk to Mr. Johnston, who owns the property. The tree does belong to him, you know. It's on his property, so it depends on what he wants to do. But if it's in the way of his building, it'll have to come down. That's what the city bylaws allow. Not much we can do one way or another."

"But you'll talk to the owner, Uncle? For sure?"

"Sure. But no guarantees. See you later, kiddo."

As he drives away, Isabelle pulls my sleeve. "I don't understand, Jeanie. What does your uncle mean?"

"You heard him, didn't you? He says it's up to the owner."

"So they can *really* cut down our tree? Like, *really*?"

"Guess so," I mumble.

"We've got to think of some way to stop them." Isabelle pounds her fist into her hand. "We've got to make them *want* to keep that tree. And a woodpecker's nest just won't cut it."

"Look. It's not *my* fault if they chop down that tree."

"Yeah, sure. But those darn developers are *your* uncle and *your* dad."

I kick at a rock. "Don't worry. I'll think of something."

"Hunh!" Isabelle says. "You better. Or else!"

Chapter 8

THAT NIGHT AT SUPPER, I can't wait to ask Dad about the tree again.

When I do, he shakes his head. "We talked about it and Berny said it all depends on the owner. If a tree's on someone's land, it's his tree. If it's in the way of the new house, it'll have to come down. Nothing we can do about it."

"But . . . but it's such a big beautiful old tree, Dad. Isabelle says it's a cedar! And it's been growing there for years and years. Centuries, even. I bet it was there even before the school was built."

"Probably long before that. Whole forests of trees like that one grew around here before loggers cut them down."

"They needed room to build the city," Mom says. "Some people think trees just block the view." She glances up at a high window above the kitchen table. Thick green ferns block most of the light. "Do you remember the beautiful view we had from our dining room in Sandberg? You could see way out into the fields with no trees or shrubs blocking it. And that huge blue prairie sky . . . Not a cloud in sight . . ." She sighs.

"Talking about views," I say. "From the top of the cedar, you can see the *whole city*! And Isabelle says on a clear day, you can even see lights on the chairlift across the inlet."

"The top?" Mom looks horrified. "You didn't climb to the top of that tall tree, did you? What if you fell? You'd break your neck."

"No, we didn't really go to the top. And it's not so dangerous. There are lots of branches to hold onto. We stayed right near the trunk and held on tight and we were very careful. Some kids even built a tree fort."

Mom shakes her head and her silver earrings jangle. Before she forbids me from climbing, I realize I'd better change the subject. Fast.

"I'm going to be in the chorus for the winter musical we're having at school before the holidays," I announce.

"That's what you said last night. That's just great!" Mom smiles at me. "I'm glad you're getting involved in school activities. It's the best way to make new friends."

"I sure miss Josie, though, Mom."

"I know, sweetie. I miss my friends too. Maybe we'll be able to go back to Sandberg to visit in the summer. Now, how about homework?"

I groan. Homework. Ugh!

Chapter 9

"WHAT DID THEY SAY?" Isabelle asks the next morning when I meet her under the tree. "Will your dad and uncle talk to the owner about our tree?"

I shake my head gloomily. "My dad said the same thing as my uncle. If a tree's in the way of new construction, you're allowed to cut it down. He says there's nothing anyone can do."

"But . . . but, that's got to be against the Charter of Rights for trees!" Isabelle explodes.

All during math and language arts that morning, rain pounds the piles of rubble that used to be the small house. One good thing: the chainsaw work crew hasn't arrived to cut down the tree. Yet.

"Remember, it's our spelling test today," Mr. Grady says. "Right after recess. Now is your last chance to study."

The class groans. I stare at the words in my spelling book. There's a bunch I'm not sure about. I try to memorize them all at once. "Drat!" I mutter. I should have studied them last night instead of reading that prairie dog mystery.

At my old school, Mrs. Fan always made up neat puzzles and games with the spelling words. Then we all learned how to spell the words and had fun too.

I doodle a picture of the giant cedar on the back cover of my spelling exercise book, thinking about my friend Josie back home. She's a real artist. She would have drawn a really beautiful Christmas tree picture.

I put a star at the top and a string of lights around it. I draw a couple of woodpeckers flying around. I'm so engrossed in my drawing I jump when Isabelle pokes my arm.

"They're back!" she hisses.

A truck's stopped near the tree. It's pulling a trailer. With the excavator on it!

I gasp.

"Those darn developers!" Isabelle glares at them.

My cheeks burn. Well, Isabelle's right. I just wish those darn developers weren't my family.

The recess bell rings. I still don't know my spelling, so I grab my spelling book for some last minute cramming.

This time, both Isabelle and I quietly, slowly, carefully get our coats and quietly, slowly, carefully leave the class. Then we gallop outside like racehorses and sprint through the rain to the cedar. A bunch of other kids follows us.

"Climb the tree," Isabelle shouts. "They won't dare cut down a tree with kids in."

"Let's go!" Mojo yells. He and George swarm up the tree as fast as two monkeys. Mee-Sue is right behind them.

Isabelle leaps up and is about to swing into the tree as well, but I grab her jacket. "Wait up. That doesn't look like a chainsaw crew."

Isabelle jumps down and stares at the workmen. They start loading a pile of rubble into the back of a waiting dump truck.

"Maybe they won't be cutting the tree down yet," Mojo says from his perch above our heads. "They'll probably cart away that other stuff first. Then they'll come back later and cut it down."

"If they only knew how special this tree is, they wouldn't *dare* touch it." Isabelle's green eyes flash at me.

"Maybe we'll think of something," I mutter. I really don't believe we have any hope of saving it. If the owner wants to cut the tree down, he will. That's what both Uncle Berny and Dad say. How can a bunch of kids stop some developers? Even if those developers are one of the kids' relatives.

I couldn't even stop my family from moving away from Sandberg to Vancouver. Though I sure did try.

The other kids climb down from the tree and go off to play soccer.

"Ready for the spelling test?" I ask Isabelle.

"Guess so," she shrugs. "Mr. G. goes so slow, he practically spells the words for you."

"Want to test me?" I give her my book.

She notices my Christmas tree doodle on the back cover. "Nice picture. I didn't know you're an artist."

"I'm not. I was just doodling and thinking what a gorgeous Christmas tree this tree would be with a huge string of coloured lights and maybe a twinkling star at the top." I pat the tree's rough bark like it's a giant friendly dog.

"Jeanie!" Isabelle grabs my arm. "That's it. You've got it. A gigantic Christmas tree. We'll decorate the tree for Christmas!"

"So?" I don't get it.

"So." Isabelle stares at me like I'm a dunce. "We get a mass of lights and some huge decorations and spread them all up the tree. Then when the owner sees it, he's bound to agree that it's so absolutely, so incredibly *beautiful*, he wouldn't dare cut it down."

My heart skips a beat. Is it possible? Can we save this tree after all?

"You know what, Isabelle? It just might work! It's sure worth a try. Better than standing around waiting for the chainsaw crew to cut it down."

Isabelle's freckled cheeks flush red with excitement. "Hey! Let's do it. We could even make it a surprise. We'll light up the whole tree and everyone will be so amazed. We'll defend our dear tree to the death! I know — we'll be the *Tree Musketeers!*"

"Tree Musketeers! How do you like that, old tree?" I pat its bark again. "All for one and one for all. We'd need plenty of lights though. You got any extras at your house?"

"No, I don't think so." Isabelle shakes her head. "You?"

I shake my head too. "We used to have plenty, but we had to leave them behind in Sandberg."

"We could buy some at the mall."

"What about money? It'd take lots of lights to cover this whole tree. It's so enormous!"

"I know!" Isabelle's red hair is electric with excitement. "We'll ask the kids in the choir to bring extras from home. It's for a good cause. They'll go for it. I know they will!"

"It just might work. We'll have to get the lights soon though."

"Right. It's just a week before our concert next Friday," Isabelle says. "Wouldn't it be *so* fantastic if we got the tree ready by then? Then at the end of the concert, *boom!* We light it all up. Talk about *dramatic!*"

"You think Mr. G. would go for it?"

"Maybe. He loves dramatic things. The more dramatic, the better. He always loves putting on the musicals. Not sure how he feels about saving trees though."

The bell rings, ending recess. We have to return to class.

And the spelling test. And I still haven't studied.

I end up getting five wrong out of twenty. The worst mark in the entire class, except for Mojo's. He gets ten wrong.

Isabelle says he always does that on purpose as a protest against spelling tests.

He probably tried to get them all wrong. But by mistake, he spelled ten right.

Chapter 10

AFTER SCHOOL, THE COLD splashy rain soaks into my teddy-bear parka as usual.

I follow Isabelle dashing across the schoolyard to the tree to check how we could decorate it. Under its sheltering branches, we peer out at the big white APPLICATION FOR DEVELOPMENT sign.

I grit my teeth and pull my parka tighter. I wish I had a spray can so I could blot out that embarrassing name: Berny S. Leclare, contractor-builder.

"Don't worry, old tree," I mutter silently, patting its rough bark. "We'll save you yet."

Mojo ducks into the dry shelter under the branches

too. He stares out at the rain pounding the remaining piles of debris that used to be a house. "Dismal," he says.

"Yep," Isabelle says. "But we haven't given up on saving the tree yet."

Mojo grabs the rope and swings back and forth.

"Achoo!" Isabelle sneezes. She rifles through her pockets. "Drat! No tissue."

She rubs her nose on the back of her hand. The rain has plastered her hair into red rivulets against her freckled cheeks. She sniffs loudly and tells me, "We should get to rehearsal a bit early on Monday morning, like maybe quarter to eight. Then we can ask Mr. G. if we can talk to the kids about our Tree Musketeers plan."

"Tree Musketeers plan?" Mojo says. "What's that?"

"A plan Jeanie and I have to save this tree," Isabelle tells him.

"Fat chance," he scoffs. "There'll be no stopping those guys when they arrive with their chainsaws."

"That's what you think," Isabelle says. "We're going to decorate this tree like a gigantic Christmas tree with lights and decorations and everything. Then no one will *dare* cut it down."

"Where are you getting the lights?"

"We'll ask the kids at choir practice to bring any extras to school, by Wednesday at the latest. That'll give us two days to get them up on the tree before the musical on Friday night when we'll light it all up. It's for a good cause. I mean, the life of this old tree's at stake. Plus it'd be good for the environment."

"Hey, Mojo. You want to help us?" I ask him.

"Might," Mojo says, twirling around on the rope.

"Think the kids will go for it?" I ask.

"Maybe," he says.

"They're bound to," Isabelle says. "Every kid in school

loves this tree. I mean, who wouldn't? It's been here, like, forever."

"Hope you're right. See you Monday morning then. Same time, same station." I give the shaggy trunk one last pat and head home.

"Get here early. Remember?" Isabelle calls out to me.

"Right. I'll be there."

I'm really glad it'll be Isabelle talking to the kids in the gym on Monday morning and not me. I don't mind helping the whole cause. I *want* to, in fact. Saving that giant cedar's important. But making a speech in front of all those kids I don't even know! That would be way scary. I could never do that in a million years.

But Isabelle won't mind a bit. In fact, she'll probably *enjoy* all the extra attention.

Chapter 11

"IT'S STILL RAINING," I complain to Mom and Dad at breakfast on Saturday morning. "It's like it'll never stop in this town."

"I know," Mom agrees. She's grinding coffee beans. "Makes everything so dreary."

"But a bit of rain sure is a lot easier to work in than snow and ice," Dad says.

"Can I get a new raincoat? The rain always soaks right through my parka. The kids at school all have cool waterproof rain jackets with hoods and everything."

"You're probably right." Mom smiles at me. "If this rain doesn't stop all winter, a raincoat makes sense. And I could use some new waterproof boots."

After breakfast, we go to the mall. It's close enough to walk. We set off under umbrellas.

"Could we go past the school?" I ask. "It's not that much farther."

"Good idea." Dad nods. "Then I can show you our building project, Rose," he tells Mom.

When we get there, the giant cedar waves its arms in welcome.

"Just look at that tree, Dad. How could you even think of cutting down such a wonder?"

He stares at the swaying branches and nods. "You're right, sweetie. It's quite exceptional. But in the end, it's just a tree. I don't know what all the fuss is about."

"I told you, Dad. The kids at school are crazy about it. Look, they've tied a rope swing on it."

"A swing," he says. "Right."

I see he's not convinced. "Kids climb it all the time and there's even a tree fort up there. Want to see it?"

"No. That's fine. I believe you."

"Let's get going to the mall." Mom pulls her coat collar closer. "My feet are soaked."

"A raincoat for Jeanie and rain boots for us all," Dad says. He hooks his arm under Mom's elbow and they start walking away.

I can't think of any other argument to convince him to fight to save the tree.

Why do he and Uncle Berny have to be so destructive?

Don't they know that they're *ruining* my life? When that tree comes down, that will be the end of any chance I have of making friends around here. I'm sure Isabelle won't ever speak to me again.

I follow along, dragging my feet through the puddles. By the time we get to the mall, my feet are soaked right through.

Chapter 12

EARLY MONDAY MORNING, I gulp down a bowl of Crumbles. Dad's already dressed for work in jeans and a thick flannel shirt.

"That's all you're having for breakfast?" he asks, stirring eggs on the stove. "How about some of my delicious scrambled eggs on a toasted bagel?"

"No time. I've got choir practice. I have to get there early this morning." I pull on my new green rain jacket. "Bye, Dad."

I grab my lunch bag and scoot out the door. Jogging through the rain, I feel ten pounds lighter in my new coat. It even smells good out here this morning. Fresh, like lemons or mint.

Isabelle isn't at school yet, so I duck under the cedar to wait for her. I grab the rope and swing back and forth, in and out of the rain. Back and forth. This time I keep my singing inside, in case Mojo and his pal George are around.

My watch says 7:58. Still no Isabelle.

Maybe her mother dropped her off on the other side of the school and she's already in the gym.

I jump off the rope and sprint to the gym. I arrive breathing hard and glance at my watch. 8:02. Mr. G. glares at my clatter.

I shuck off my jacket and scan the kids on stage. Isabelle isn't there! Oh no! Something must have happened to her.

I take my place in the chorus line on stage beside Trudy, who smiles a welcome. I try to smile back, but I'm so worried, my mouth won't co-operate. I stare at the door.

Isabelle doesn't arrive. And she doesn't arrive. For the *whole practice*, she doesn't arrive . . .

My stomach flips and churns. I can't concentrate on the songs. What can I do?

If Isabelle isn't here, who will talk to the kids about our plan to save the tree?

I'll have to do it myself. There's no one else. But what can I say?

We have to get the lights by tomorrow. Or the next day, at the latest. It's our only hope. Now the fate of that tree is all up to *me*. But will the kids even listen to me?

If only Isabelle were here. She'd stand up on the stage and announce in her loud clear voice that we were all going to save the tree. And she'd raise her fist and tell everyone our plan. She'd be so convincing, all the kids would be right behind her.

Oh, hurry, Isabelle. Hurry! The tree needs you. I need you! My heart beats so hard, I'm sure Trudy can hear it.

Practice is almost over. Isabelle still isn't here.

Mr. Grady bangs out the final chorus on the piano. Then he waves at the chorus line. "Well done today, boys and girls. We're bouncing right along. We'll have another practice after recess today with the whole cast." This is the usual signal for the kids to leave.

I take a deep breath. This is my only chance. I raise my sweaty hand.

"Mr. Grady. Excuse me, Mr. Grady. Could . . . could I please ask the kids something?"

Mr. Grady's caterpillar eyebrows arch, but he nods. "Hold on there a minute, boys and girls. Before you go, our new friend Jeanie has something to ask you."

My stomach twists. I lurch forward.

What can I say? How should I start?

I stumble to the front of the mob of kids, then turn to face everyone. My mind's a total blank. Half out the door, the kids turn back and wait, staring at me.

I bite my lip and shake my head. No use. Those kids would never listen to me. They shuffle impatiently.

I swallow hard to clear my throat. I still can't think of what to say, what words to use. "Um . . ."

"Hey, you guys," Mojo pipes up. "You know that giant cedar tree beside the schoolyard with the rope swing?"

"Course," George says. "Only decent climbing tree around."

The kids stop fidgeting to listen.

"Well, some developer's gonna chop it down," Mojo says.

"No! They can't do that!"

"So some of us got to thinking about a way to *save* that tree. To *defend* it." Mojo goes on, hands in his jeans pockets. He lowers his voice now, like he's letting the kids in on a secret. Everyone's eyes are glued to him. "Here's our plan. We're going to plaster the whole thing with decorations and lights like some humungous Christmas tree. And we'll send a petition to the owner to tell him that he *can't* cut it down."

"So where are you getting all the lights and stuff?" George asks.

"Glad you ask, bud." Mojo's eyes flash. "That's where all you guys come in."

He points to the kids. "We need plenty of lights. And plenty of decorations. Big ones. So we're asking you to bring in any extra outdoor lights you have at home and we'll string them all together and hang them on the tree. Right, Jeanie?"

I nod at him. I try to smile. My cheeks are frozen as stiff as ice cubes. I still haven't found my voice.

Mojo goes on. "Also, I was thinking we could have a bake sale to raise money for some extra lights and stuff. And I'll help sell the cookies because you always get free samples. I just *love* bake sales!" He arches his eyebrows.

The kids laugh.

He goes on in his loud voice. "Anyway, we need the lights and stuff for the tree soon. Like tomorrow morning. No later."

The kids all talk at once. "Tomorrow! That's not enough time."

"A bake sale! Yeah! Mojo's right. We'll have to advertise and everything."

"We can make up some signs today so kids will know to bring money for the cookies tomorrow, and we could ask the office to announce it on the P.A."

"And we'll make cookies at home tonight after school. Sure. We can do it!"

"Could we have a bake sale at recess tomorrow, Mr. G.?" Trudy asks. "Would you sponsor us?"

"Fine." Mr. Grady nods. "Saving that big tree sounds like a worthwhile project."

"Great! Who'll make the signs?" Trudy says.

"Our class has art before recess today. Let's ask if we can make them then."

"All right!" Mojo shouts, raising his fist. "Tree Musketeers! Let's go!"

The kids raise their fists too. "All for one and one for all!" they shout.

Finally, I find my voice. I shout with them and raise my fist too.

Although my knees are shaking and my throat's dry, I'm suddenly so relieved I feel like hugging all those smiling, shouting kids.

Even Mojo.

Chapter 13

BY LUNCHTIME, the hallways are plastered with signs: "Save our giant tree, giant bake sale. Buy a cookie. Buy a dozen. Sign our petition. Recess tomorrow. Help save our tree!"

Trudy and I are taping the last signs to a wall when Isabelle arrives.

She says in a breathless, croaky voice, "Bad cold, but I told my mom I just *had* to come to school today. I kept bugging her until she finally let me come this afternoon. What's this about a bake sale?"

The bell rings, so we shuffle up to our classroom, carried along by the crowd while I explain.

"The bake sale is Mojo's idea to raise extra money for some Christmas lights if we don't get enough donations. But lots of kids say they'll bring lights and cookies for the sale to our practice tomorrow morning."

"Fantastic! I knew you could do it. And all these signs!" Isabelle croaks and grins broadly at me. "Looking good!"

"Actually, Mojo did the talking," I admit. "Which is good, because you know how the kids always listen to him."

"Oh, that guy! He's such a show-off," Isabelle sniffs. "But I'm glad he's on our side for once."

"Me too." I grin back.

Maybe our plan will work. Maybe we'll stop Leclare Construction from destroying that tree. Tree Musketeers! *All for one and one for all!*

And maybe, just maybe, Isabelle will be my friend after all.

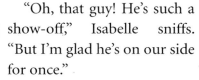

Next morning, I'm up in the tree waiting for Isabelle. I straddle the lowest branch and bounce up and down impatiently. It's like riding a slow-moving farm horse. My grandmother has a big old horse she calls Jake that my cousins and I ride around the farmyard in the summer.

"Hurry, Isabelle. Hurry, Isabelle," I chant in time with the bouncing.

It's a soothing tree. The branches sway and drift around me. Yet I feel the solid trunk reaching down with its roots, down into the ground, holding the whole sweet-smelling tree so firmly, so sturdily that it could stand right here forever.

"Dear sweet tree," I whisper. "How wonderful you are."

There's Isabelle at last. I jump down and land with a thud at her feet.

"Hi, you," Isabelle grins at me. "Remember your cookies?"

"Course," I say as we jog to the gym. "Cornflake squares in my backpack."

At practice, lots of kids give us their bags and boxes of cookies. But only a few have any extra lights they could donate to the cause. When we string all the lights together, we see it won't be long enough. The tree's so tall, it'll need plenty of lights.

Mojo says, "I couldn't bring cookies because my mom had to work the night shift at the hospital last night. So I got the petition ready. And I'll help you sell the stuff at recess. Any free samples?" He peeks inside a bag.

"Paws off!" Isabelle grabs the bag from him. "No free samples."

* * *

Recess is amazing! Kids swarm the sale tables like an army of starving ants.

"Twenty-five cents each?"

"Right. Fifty cents for two. And you have to sign our petition about saving the tree." Mojo sticks his petition in front of each customer.

When the bell rings, ending recess, every cookie and square has vanished and we've collected a cookie tin full of coins. While we clean up the crumbs, Mojo counts the signatures on the petition.

"Zoo-ie!" he says, flipping the pages. "A hundred and seventy-nine signatures!"

"I'll take that," Isabelle says. "Thanks, Mojo." She turns to me. "Hey, Jeanie. Can you come and deliver the petition to the owner with me after school? Then we can go to the mall to buy the lights."

"Sure."

It's for a good cause. I'm sure my mom won't mind.

Chapter 14

AFTER SCHOOL ON OUR way to the mall, we stop at the owner's apartment. Isabelle found his address in the phone book at the office when we went to call my mom about being late. We want to deliver the petition in person so we can explain to the owner how we feel about the tree. At the front door of the apartment building, Isabelle pushes the button next to his name. D. Johnston, in apartment 306.

"Hello?" An elderly woman's voice comes through the static.

"Hello. Could we see Mr. Johnston, please?"

"Mr. Johnston? Sorry, he's not home now."

"Oh."

We didn't think that he wouldn't be there.

"Um," Isabelle says. "We have something for him. A petition. Could we bring it up?"

"A fish delivery for Mr. Johnston?"

"No, a petition," Isabelle says louder into the intercom.

"Okay. I'll push the button and you can come up. We're on the third floor."

"Fish?" Isabelle screws up her face at me. "Where'd she get that idea?"

The door buzzes. I shrug and enter the lobby. Isabelle follows me inside.

We take the elevator to the third floor. When we knock, a friendly-looking elderly woman opens the door. A wave of deliciousness hits me. Ginger cookies.

"Come in," the woman says. She's wearing a pink polka-dotted scarf around her curly grey hair, and a matching pink polka-dotted apron.

Isabelle shows her the petition and explains how it's about the cedar tree next to the school.

"Oh," the woman says. "That's what you've come for. I thought you were our fish delivery. That intercom really needs fixing. There's so much static. Sorry, but I can't help you, girls. My husband won't be home until this evening. How would you like a cookie? I've just taken a batch of gingerbread out of the oven."

The cookies are melt-in-your-mouth delicious, but

Isabelle's still bent on trying to explain about our petition.

"We have all these names of people who want to save that cedar tree."

The woman shakes her head and won't even look at the petition.

"But it's really important . . ." Isabelle's cheeks grow red with frustration as she waves the sheets of paper in front of the woman's face.

"I'm really sorry, dear." The woman smiles at us. "My husband is looking after that building project. Now, I'll just put a couple of these cookies into a bag for you."

Finally, Isabelle gives up and puts the petition back into her jacket pocket. We say goodbye and head for the elevator with our cookies. On our way down, Isabelle's face is still red with frustration.

"She was nice," I say, munching a cookie. "Maybe we should have left the petition with her to give to Mr. Johnston."

"She'd probably just wrap her fish in it."

"Fish?" A bubble of laughter bursts out of my mouth.

Isabelle stares at me. Then she starts laughing too. We both giggle the rest of the way to the mall.

Chapter 15

ALTHOUGH IT'S MORE than a week before Christmas, the mall is buzzing with frantic shoppers. We rush straight to the department store. After asking for directions to the Christmas lights, we find them in the Dress Your Tree department on the second floor.

"Holy crow! Look at these prices!" Isabelle says. "We don't have that kind of money."

"But what about saving the tree?" I ask.

"I don't know. We'll think of something else. We *have* to! It's too late for another bake sale. Maybe our Tree Musketeers plan is doomed."

We dejectedly thread our way through the crowds and start for home.

As we trudge past Wong's Second-Hand shop, I notice some dusty Christmas decorations jumbled in the front window.

"Think we could find anything in here?"

"You're right. Maybe Mrs. Wong has some Christmas lights." Isabelle turns into the shop.

"Wouldn't hurt to ask, I guess." I follow Isabelle. But I must admit, I'm not feeling very hopeful.

"Oh yes. I have a long, long string of outdoor lights," Mrs. Wong says when we find her. "A big bunch. What do you want them for, girls? You have a big house?"

"No," Isabelle says. "There's a tree beside our school we want to decorate. Maybe you've noticed it? A huge old cedar? We're trying to stop them from chopping it down."

"I know that tree. They can't really be thinking of cutting it down. It's been there forever. Oh, those nasty developers! Destroying our neighbourhood. And what about the environment?"

"They want to build a big house there, but we have to show them that tree is too beautiful and important to destroy," Isabelle goes on.

My neck prickles uncomfortably. After all, my father and uncle are developers. In fact, they're the *very* ones planning to chop the tree down! But then I remember. I'm mad at them, anyway.

"Do you think these lights will do?" Mrs. Wong shows us an enormous bundle of coloured outdoor lights.

"They'd be perfect!" Isabelle grins. "But how much are they?"

When she tells us, I'm glad we have enough money.

"Just a minute, girls. I have something else you might be able to use."

The woman disappears into the back of her cluttered shop. She soon reappears lugging a very large yellow plastic star that comes almost to her waist. It's a bit dusty and its wires are a tangled mess.

"Perfect for the top!" Isabelle says.

I nod.

"Let's check if it still works." Mrs. Wong finds the plug and pushes it into a wall socket.

The star lights up with twinkling LED bulbs inside.

"It's terrific!" Isabelle says. "We can tie it to the treetop and it'll look magic."

"I doubt if we can afford it. After paying for the lights, we'll have only three dollars left," I say, quickly subtracting in my head.

"Funny," Mrs. Wong says, smiling at us. "That's exactly the price of this star."

"Oh, that's lucky." Isabelle gives her the rest of the bake sale money.

After thanking Mrs. Wong, we carry the lights and star away in two giant garbage bags.

"Look at the time!" I say. "I've got to get home. Mom will be so worried."

"But when can we put up the lights?" Isabelle says. "The musical's the day after tomorrow."

"How about after school tomorrow? I could store them at my place until then. And maybe you could take the star?"

"Okay. Tomorrow. For sure."

Chapter 16

AFTER SCHOOL THE next day, I race home for the lights
— those we bought as well as the strings donated by the
kids in choir. Mom isn't home, so I don't have to waste
time explaining our plan. I leave a quick note for her on
the fridge that I have to go back to school for something.
Then I sprint back to the tree, lugging the plastic garbage
bag of lights.

Isabelle is standing impatiently beside the star in a big
bag. "I thought you'd never get here, Jeanie."

The school grounds are deserted and it's already getting dark. "Where's everyone else?" I ask. "Where's Mojo?"

"Said he had a dentist appointment or something."

"I was hoping at least a couple other kids would be

here to help us decorate the tree." I'm not keen on climbing the tree, loaded down with lights, in this weather. In *any* weather, actually.

"Guess we forgot to tell anyone else that we'd be putting up the lights after school," Isabelle says. "Maybe some kids will come by later. Anyways, who needs them? We can do it ourselves. No prob. I'll climb the tree and you can hand the lights up to me."

"All right," I say, raising my eyebrows.

Isabelle's got some good ideas. But she sure can be bossy. As bossy as Athos in *The Three Musketeers*.

She swings up into the tree and reaches down for the lights. I pass up the heavy bundle. Then I follow her into the tree, sticking close to the broad trunk where I feel safest. Before we've gone far, someone else arrives. It's Mojo.

"Hey," he calls up to us. "You guys started without me."

"Thought you had a dentist appointment," Isabelle calls down.

"Turns out it's not until five o'clock," he says. "So I can help you for a while. Want me to bring up the rest of these lights?"

"No, Jeanie and I will get these up. But you can untangle the wires in the star. Then Jeanie will hand it up to me after we've got this set of lights up."

He dumps the star out of the plastic garbage bag. "Woo-ie!" he says. "Now that's what I call a real mess." He starts untangling the wires.

Meanwhile, Isabelle and I take turns climbing and

passing up the bundle of lights higher and higher. We string them up the trunk, and Isabelle attaches them out along each swaying branch as far as she can reach. The lights make a crooked path toward the top. Past the rope swing, past the tree fort, all the way up to the empty woodpecker's nest.

"Now for the star," Isabelle says, on our way back down. "It'll look so cool at the very top."

"Right." As long as I don't have to climb to the top, I tell myself. Up there, the trunk's so thin, it could snap right off under my weight. I have to bite my bottom lip to stop it from trembling. And my stomach's bouncing around like a bird's in there, frantically trying to get out.

"Okey-dokey," Mojo says as we land beside him. "This star's all ready to fly."

"You mean you untangled all those wires already?" Isabelle's clearly impressed.

"It's what I do." Mojo grins in her direction.

"Great," she says. "Maybe you can untangle the wires for those other lights and get them all set to go up the tree as well."

"No prob," he says, dumping the rest of the lights out of the plastic garbage bag. "But after this, I've got to go. Don't want to miss that dentist appointment."

"Okay, Jeanie. I'll climb to the first branch and you can pass the star up to me," Isabelle directs in her usual bossy manner as she swings up into the tree.

Grunting, I try to lift the heavy star to her.

"Higher," she directs from the branch above my head. "I can't reach it yet."

Mojo gives me a hand to heave the star up higher until she can grab it.

"Thanks," I mutter to him. "You want to climb up there?"

"Sorry," he says. "Not enough time. Got to make tracks now."

"Okay. See you later."

I sure wish Mojo could be the one climbing to the top of the tree with Isabelle and that heavy star. But he can't, so it'll have to be me. And I know if I say anything, Isabelle will know I'm chicken, and that would ruin everything. She'd never want a friend who's a scaredy-cat. So I swing up to the branch beside her.

"I'll go a bit higher and you can pass it up again," she tells me.

We climb slowly, lugging the heavy star, up past all the lights. Up and up. The higher we go, the louder the wind whistles through the branches. Now the trunk is as narrow as one of my legs and the tree is swaying back and forth.

Is it warning us not to go any higher?

"Um, Isabelle," I stammer, my teeth chattering. "Aren't we high enough?"

I can't let her think I'm chicken. But it sure is scary way up here.

"Think so? I'll go up to just this next branch. Then you can pass me the star again."

"Okay. But be careful." Now my voice is shaking too. I don't dare glance down. The ground's miles away.

Isabelle eases up higher. And higher.

The treetop sways dizzily, and the wind whispers through the branches. *Unsafe. Too high*, it hisses. *Go down. Down. Down . . .*

I gulp hard, wrapping one arm around the slim trunk and lean into it.

"I'll pass you the star now. This is high enough, right?" I try to sound as brave as a Musketeer. But my voice ends in a squeak.

"But it's not the top yet."

"It doesn't have to be the very top."

Isabelle's feet are above my head. That means I'll have to climb even higher to lift the star to her.

"Okay, okay. Hand it to me. I'll tie it here. Can't you hold it steady?"

"I . . . I'll try."

I catch my breath and ease the heavy star even higher, holding it as steady as I can.

Maybe if I shut my eyes, it won't be so scary. But the wind is strong and my stomach dips, so I snap them back open. Eyes shut at the top of a swaying cedar on a windy night is definitely petrifying.

"I'll just wind the wires around this branch," Isabelle says. "There. That should hold it."

How can she be so calm? Isn't she even a *bit* scared?

"All right," she says. "Let's climb back down now."

The trip down is even harder. Going backward in the dark, it's impossible to see the footholds.

Hugging the trunk, I mutter, "Come on. You can do it. You can do it." I feel for a safe branch. My foot connects. I lower myself. Down and down.

Finally, I reach the lowest branches and swing onto the soft ground. I rub my wobbly legs. Mojo's gone now. He left the rest of the lights in a long string at the base of the tree.

"Imagine how amazed everyone will be tomorrow night when we turn these babies on!" Isabelle says as she leaps down beside me. "All those lights. And that star! I can hardly wait to try them out."

"What about the rest of the lights?" I ask, pointing to the ones Mojo left for us.

"We'll use those for the lower branches."

So back up the tree we go. It turns out there aren't a lot of lights, so it doesn't take long to spread them out along the lower branches.

When we're finished, we drop down onto the ground beside the tree. Before we can stand back and admire our job, a white van turns up the street. It stops in front of the property. Leclare Brothers Construction.

Chapter 17

"YOUR UNCLE!" Isabelle squeals. "Let's ask him for a ride home. Then we can tell him to bring Mr. Johnston to our concert tomorrow night."

Oh? I didn't know *that* was part of the plan.

"Uncle Berny!" I yell. "Uncle Berny!"

He gets out of the van and saunters toward us, holding his baseball cap down in the wind. "Hey, what's happening, kiddo?" he says in his big cheery voice. "You two on tree guard duty?"

"Ha ha!" I say. "Can you give me and my friend, Isabelle, a ride home?"

"Sure thing. Hop in. I'm just picking up some tools, and then I'll be right there."

I climb into the front seat, kicking a thick roll of red plastic tape off a coil of yellow extension cord. An idea pops into my head.

"Decorations!" I tell Isabelle. "Bright red decorations for our Christmas tree!"

"Now you're talking," she says, nodding. She sniffs and rubs her nose on the back of her hand.

"Um, Uncle," I say, when he climbs into the van and starts it up. "This roll of red plastic tape. Could we have it? Please?"

"Now what would you kids want that for?"

"For a . . . special project. A sort-of special school project. It'd be perfect!"

"Well, if it's for school, all right."

"Another thing, Uncle Berny. Can you bring the owner, what's his name?"

"Mr. Johnston," Isabelle reminds me.

"Right. Can you bring him to our school concert tomorrow night? It's going to be really good."

"Tell him we'll have a special surprise for him," Isabelle says.

"Hmm, a surprise, eh? Wonder what you two are cooking up. Fine, I'll do my best, but I'm warning you: Mr. Johnston is set in his ways. I don't know how he feels about school concerts."

"But it's really, really, *really* important for him to come, Uncle."

"I almost forgot," Isabelle says, rummaging in her jacket pocket. "Here's a petition for him from the kids at school about the tree. We got almost two hundred signatures. Could you give it to him?"

"Sure. But I don't know if it'll do any good. Now where do you live, Isabelle?"

When we get to Isabelle's house, Uncle Berny says, "Before you go, I should show you two this."

He pulls a cardboard tube from the dashboard. "Here are the plans for Mr. Johnston's new house," he explains. He flicks on the cab lights and unrolls a thick paper from the tube. "This square is where the new house will be built." Then he points to another smaller square at the edge of the paper. "And right here is where the garage will be. I'm sorry to say, that's right, smack, where your cedar tree is."

I stare at the blue lines and my heart sinks. I blink hard. I see *exactly* what he means. To make way for the new garage, our tree will have to be removed after all.

But Isabelle isn't the least bit worried. "They'll just have to put the garage somewhere else," she says breezily. "They can't cut down our tree. They just *can't*. And that's that." She sniffs again.

"As I said, I'll talk to the owner." Uncle Berny shrugs. "But, as you can see, we've got a problem."

We walk with Isabelle into the house because it's dark out and her mom's car isn't there. Uncle Berny is reluctant to leave Isabelle alone.

"I always get home before my mom," she insists. "She'll be here by six after she picks up my little brother from daycare. Really. She will."

After we turn on all the lights in the living room and kitchen, Uncle Berny finally agrees to leave her.

"Spunky kid," he says as we drive away.

Spunky! That's Isabelle, all right. She's afraid of nothing. And because of her and our Tree Musketeers project, I've almost forgotten about missing Sandberg. Almost.

I stare out at the wet streets and the colourful Christmas lights decorating the houses. It's hard to believe Christmas is just a week away and there isn't a single flake of snow anywhere.

That night after supper, I work at the kitchen table, using up the whole roll of my uncle's plastic tape tying large red bows onto long pipe cleaners from my craft box. My plan is that we'll use the wires to fasten the bows to the tree.

"What are those for?" Mom asks, glancing up from the TV.

She's folding a basket of clothes into piles on the coffee table while she and Dad watch a movie so old it's in black and white. Something about Christmas and angels. I'm too busy to watch it.

"They're for a school project, sort of," I say, stuffing the bows into a garbage bag to take to school tomorrow.

I haven't figured out just *when* we'll attach the bows onto the tree. But I'm sure Isabelle will come up with a plan. She always does.

Chapter 18

EARLY THE NEXT morning, the day of the musical, I wait impatiently for Isabelle under the tree.

It's a misty morning, like in our play *Santa Lost in Mish-Mash Land*. Perfect weather to put everyone in the right mood for the show tonight.

Also, with this weather, no one will notice the lights and star on the tree. So our secret will be safe until we turn them on at *exactly* the right moment for the great surprise.

But what if Uncle Berny can't convince Mr. Johnston to come to the musical?

I pace around the tree, dragging the plastic garbage bag filled with my plastic decorations. Isabelle's late again. I'm about to give up when she finally arrives, her purple rain-coat flapping behind her.

"Bad news," she croaks. "Laryngitis."

"Oh no! How can you sing tonight?"

Isabelle shrugs. "Hope Mr. G. comes up with some-thing. The show must go on, because of you-know-what." She looks back at our friend, the giant cedar.

* * *

"Me? No way!" I shake my head at Mr. Grady's suggestion. "Up on stage? Like, all by *myself*? In front of all those strangers? I couldn't. I just couldn't. I can't sing!"

"Sure she can." Mojo grins at me. "She's a real good singer. I heard her out there by the tree last week. Singing loud as a famous opera star."

George nods. "I heard her too."

I glare at them, but Mojo grins back even wider until his brown face is one big mouthful of grinning teeth.

"You won't ever be alone, Jeanie," Mr. Grady says. "Mojo's on stage most of the time. Isabelle can still do the dancing. It'll be a Biggy-Big-Ears team. Might even be effective. I heard about your performance of Wendy in *Peter Pan* at your old school. This is not so different. How about giving it a try?"

Isabelle nods at me vigorously.

"All right. I guess."

Because of the tree, I know the show must go on.

"Great! Let's try 'Surfin' Santa.' From the top now." Mr. G. pounds out the tune on the piano.

The songs are familiar now since Isabelle and her friends are always practising them. I try to remember to pull my breath deep into my chest and open my mouth really wide to let the sound out, as Mrs. Fan taught us at my old school.

"Just as I suspected. You have a great voice, Jeanie, and excellent projection." Mr. Grady nods from the piano. "You'll do just fine. Now let's get you a costume and we'll try it together."

Mrs. Honey, who helps with costumes and backstage directions, gets another Biggy-Big-Ears costume. Brown fleece sleepers, the kind little kids wear, with the feet cut out.

My stomach is whirling as I pull on the sleepers over my jeans and zip up the front. It's prickly under my arms. "Here are your ears." Mrs. Honey gives Isabelle and me each two huge plastic ears with a hairband to keep them in place over our own ears. They're about the size of my hand and they wobble around whenever we move. They probably look goofy, but at this point, who cares?

The ears tickle at first, but once I start singing, I forget about them.

During the practice, I see that my actual singing is two parts, at the beginning of the play and at the end. In the first scene, Santa/Mojo and Biggy-Big-Ears are jogging one foggy morning, trying to get fit before their long trip delivering gifts on Christmas Eve.

In the last scene, Biggy-Big-Ears, a.k.a. Isabelle/me, finally finds Santa, who has become lost. Because of our big ears and excellent hearing, we can hear the noisy holiday preparations and music, so we are able to lead Santa home triumphantly.

After several welcome home songs, the choir sings "O Christmas Tree" as Biggy-Big-Ears leads Santa and the other Mish-Mash characters around the twinkling Christmas tree on stage as a grand finale.

We try out the Biggy-Big-Ears team with Isabelle dancing and me singing. After a few miscues, we get it right and Mr. Grady says it'll do.

"Okay, everyone," he says as we finish our last practice. "Be here *promptly* at six-fifteen tonight, backstage in the dressing rooms for costumes and makeup. Don't *any* of you *dare* be late."

Isabelle drags me to the piano. "Mr. G.?" she croaks. "Could Jeanie and I talk to you about something *very important*?"

Mr. Grady's eyebrows shoot up. "Now what?" he sighs.

"Tonight, do you think," Isabelle puts a hand to her throat. "*You* ask, Jeanie," she croaks, pushing me forward. "You know, about the tree."

"Right." I take a deep breath and plunge. "Isabelle and I, we were thinking that at the end of the concert . . . Well, remember that big cedar tree out there we told you about?"

"Oh, yes. How's your project going?"

"We've put up the strings of lights. And it'll have decorations and . . . and . . ."

Mr. Grady drums his fingers on the top of the piano impatiently. Isabelle nudges me. I go on in a rush.

"My uncle's asking the property owner to come to the concert. So we're wondering if, at the end, you know, when we sing 'O Christmas Tree,' if we could all go outside. Like the audience and the cast and everyone, and see the giant Christmas tree, you know, with the lights on and the decorations and everyone could see it and . . . and . . ."

"And the owner will realize the tree's too beautiful to cut down," Mr. Grady finishes. "I see. A grand procession. With everyone singing. Hmm. Don't see why not. Sounds as if it might be a great finale for our musical. Quite dramatic, in fact. You could announce it, Jeanie. Your voice carries well. And you and Isabelle and Mojo could lead everyone outside while I play the piano. Yes. That could make a dramatic finale."

"Oh, thank you, Mr. Grady! Thank you!" The birds in my stomach are doing cartwheels.

Mr. Grady nods and almost smiles at me.

"Now, Isabelle. You take it easy. No more hanging around trees in rainstorms."

Chapter 19

THE TIME AT SCHOOL DRAGS. It's a strange misty day. Around noon, a thicker fog silently drifts in over the mist, muffling city sounds. After lunch, Mr. Grady has a good long session reading to us from *The Three Musketeers*.

By three o'clock, when school's out, the fog's so thick, I can barely see across the school grounds. "Our" cedar tree is a dark grey silhouette suspended in the lighter grey of swirling fog.

"You got the bows?" Isabelle whispers.

"Yes. In a big garbage bag behind my coat."

I follow her outside, lugging the garbage bag of Christmas bows.

No one else is around. At least we can't see anyone with this thick fog. Guess everyone's gone home to get ready for the concert tonight. We'll have to hurry.

I swing up into the tree. It's easier to climb now. It's as if the branches are reaching out to lift me, the way my grandfather used to hold out his arms to lift me to ride up on his shoulders.

Isabelle passes the bag of bows up to me and swings into the tree beside me. We attach them with the pipe-cleaners onto each branch as far out as we dare reach. We climb only as high as the woodpecker's hole, where we've attached the star cord to the light cord.

I check the connection. Everything's solid.

"Okay, old tree," I whisper. "Now it's time to do your stuff." And I slither down the trunk after Isabelle. "Should we try out the lights?" I ask. "Check how the tree will look tonight?"

"Sure. But I've just had a terrible thought, Jeanie."

"What?"

"This extension cord. There's no way it'll reach all the way into the school to plug it in. Look. When we lay it out, it doesn't go even halfway across the playground."

"Oh, rats! Why didn't we think of checking that before?"

"Maybe there's a closer electrical outlet next door. Near the tool shed, maybe?"

We find an outlet, all right, but no way will our extension cord reach that either.

"All this for nothing!" Isabelle croaks. "I can't *believe* it! The star, the lights, the bows. Getting Mr. G. to agree to lead the audience out here. For what? Nothing! With the dark, plus this blanket of fog, no one will see a thing. Just one big old dripping tree. So much for being Tree Musketeers. It's one big bust. We're doomed!" Her voice cracks. "Our tree's doomed!"

"We'll think of something, Isabelle. We've got to!" I try to swallow a lump in my throat. "The Three Musketeers never give up. Remember: all for one and one for all. And we're the *Tree* Musketeers. There *must* be something we can do. Anyway, we have to go home now so we can be back by six-fifteen for the concert."

"Okay. See you then." Isabelle trudges away dejectedly into the swirling fog.

I head home in the other direction. My feet are two heavy bricks.

* * *

"What's the matter, Jeanie?" Mom asks as I dawdle over the chicken stew. "You don't look very happy. Aren't you excited about the musical tonight?"

"Oh, Mom! It's just that, just that . . ." I almost tell her about our Tree Musketeers plan, but remember that it's a secret. I bite my lip.

Then I ask, although I already know the answer, "Do we have an extra extension cord? A really long one?"

"No. Sorry. Why do you need an extension cord?"

"It's for . . . for our school project, sort of," I finish lamely.

"Sorry," Mom says again. "Eat your stew now before it gets cold. You don't want to be late for the concert."

"Are you and Dad coming?"

"Of course we are, sweetie. We'll be right in the front row cheering for you."

Chapter 20

THIS TIME, ISABELLE is waiting for me under our tree. She's shuffling back and forth excitedly.

"I've got it!" she says in a husky whisper. "I know where we can get a good long extension cord."

"Where?"

"From your uncle! Carpenters *always* have them. To run their power tools and stuff."

"You're right!" My heart skips a hopeful beat. "Just hope he gets here early enough to ask him."

In the dressing room, we yank on the identical Biggy-Big-Ear furry costumes and pull on our gigantic ears. While the other girls plaster on stage makeup to make them look like various monsters and ghouls, Isabelle and I wait for Uncle Berny at the gym's entrance.

"Uncle Berny. Where are you?" I mutter as we pace back and forth.

But when Mr. Grady sees us, he shoos us backstage. "Just ten minutes to curtain time. Get into your places,

boys and girls." He claps at us, his caterpillar eyebrows wobbling wildly.

The kids buzz with excitement. They shove each other around, practise their hip-hop dance steps, and chant the beginning rap:

"Once, one day in the North,
in rolled a nasty old fog.
That was the day our Santa,
he up and went for a jog . . ."

My heart's pounding as I peek out the curtain to check again if my uncle's arrived. Mom and Dad are there, right in the front row. Mom waves and Dad's glasses glint as he smiles up at me. I wave back and look around at the audience. The chairs are filling up.

But still no Uncle Berny.

What can Isabelle and I do? Maybe my uncle won't even come. Maybe he couldn't talk our tree's owner into coming. Maybe we've decorated the tree for nothing.

Maybe, as Isabelle says, the Tree Musketeers are doomed after all.

And so is our tree.

* * *

At seven on the dot, Mr. Grady plays a loud chord on the piano and the long curtains swish open. His wide mouth stretches to remind us to smile.

"Welcome. We say welcome. Welcome to our show!" My heart's thumping as I stand beside Isabelle with the choir and sing out to the audience.

What if I forget the words? Crazy. I can sing them in my sleep.

There at the back of the audience, I see him. Uncle Berny!

He's guiding an elderly gentleman to a seat near the middle aisle! He flashes a thumbs-up sign as he sits down beside the man.

"My uncle's here!" I whisper to Isabelle, as the curtains close and everyone shuffles to their places for the next scene. "And I think he's got that Mr. Johnston with him!"

Isabelle doesn't have time to reply before the curtains slide open again.

It's the scene where Biggy-Big-Ears and Santa do a jogging sort-of hip-hop dance around the stage. As we rehearsed, Isabelle dances while I sing the duet with Santa/Mojo in his red suit and shaggy white beard.

Then while Isabelle and Mojo whiz and twirl to whirlwind music, I sing the rap, "Joggin' and Jammin'." I almost forget our problems. About how we can't find an extension cord for those Christmas lights to light up the big cedar for the grand finale. And about how our plan to save the tree is all one dismal failure.

I link arms with Isabelle and together we exit behind the big snowbank, leaving Santa lost in the swirling fog.

Now we don't have to be back on stage again until the last scene, when our Biggy-Big-Ears duo leads Santa back home safely to the North Pole.

"Well done, girls," Mrs. Honey says backstage, patting our sweaty furry backs. "You can wait in the dressing room until we call you for the last scene."

On the way down the darkened stairs, Isabelle has a big coughing fit. I help her to the dressing room and get her a drink of water.

Isabelle yanks off her big ears and takes a big gulp of water. Finally she stops coughing. "Thanks," she croaks. "That's better." She takes another gulp of water and clears her throat. "Man, that was cool! You saw your uncle? And Mr. Johnston's with him?"

I nod glumly, tugging at my sweaty armpits. "They're here, all right. But they came too late for us to ask to borrow an extension cord."

"Yeah." She slumps onto a bench. Now she's dejected too. "You must admit, it *was* a good idea while it lasted. The lights and star and everything. Too bad it's not going to work. Our Tree Musketeers plan is one big *bust!*" She kicks at the cement wall.

"Hold on!" I squeal. "I just thought of something!"

"What?"

"About your idea to get an extension cord from my uncle. Remember when he gave us a ride last night? That roll of plastic tape he gave us, you know, for the decorations?"

"So?"

"I'm sure there was an extension cord under it in his van."

Isabelle's green eyes flash. "You're thinking maybe it's *still* in the van? And we could borrow it and plug in the Christmas tree lights right now? Then hurry back here like crazy for the last act when we have to be on stage again?"

"You got it!" I nod vigorously. "Except I'll go alone. It's so dark and cold out there, you'll get pneumonia."

"No way. Where you go, I go. All for one and one for all. So what are we waiting for? Tree Musketeers. Let's go!"

Chapter 21

ISABELLE SNAPS HER gigantic ears back on and rushes for the fire exit.

I'm right behind her. I prop the door open with a rock. Then I sprint to catch up with her, bounding out into the swirling fog.

"Now where's that van?" she pants.

"There it is! In the driveway next door, near the tool shed."

We race to the van. I grab the door handle. It's locked.

Isabelle dashes to the other side. Driver's door's locked too. And so is the rear door!

"Drat!" Isabelle says.

I peer inside. The yellow extension cord is still in a big coil on the floor.

"Drat! Drat! Double drat!" I kick a tire.

"Just a minute," Isabelle says. "This window's open a bit. Your arm's skinnier. I bet you can get it through and reach the lock."

I wiggle my fingers into the crack and try to pull the window down. It moves a fraction. Enough so I can squeeze my arm inside to reach the lock.

Yes! I catch it between my fingers and pull it up.

I barely get my arm out before Isabelle yanks the door open.

I grab the extension from the floor.

I feel guilty. But I'm sure, *positive*, in fact, that Uncle Berny would understand. If we'd had time to ask him, he'd have let us borrow his cord. For *sure*.

Besides, it's for a good cause. A *very* good cause.

We sprint to the tree. Isabelle leans against the trunk, coughing and wheezing.

"All right," she pants. "You climb up and plug the extension into the lights. I'll run this end out to the shed and plug it in there. Oh, I just hope, hope, hope it works."

"It will," I say, with more confidence than I feel.

Breathing hard, I swing up into the tree, the cord between my teeth like Tarzan. As I scramble upward, my feet automatically find the branches. It's as if they shift for me.

Like magic, the tree lifts me up and up into the darkness to where I think the end of the light cord is. I feel around the trunk for it.

There it is. I plug it in, good and solid.

"Now, old tree." I pat its trunk. "Now it's up to you to show your stuff."

Slithering back down the trunk, I feel the tree whispering its thanks. As I swing down onto the spongy ground, the fog blazes into a soft pink.

Great! Isabelle must have found a plug in the tool shed.

Through the fog drifts the chorus of "Merry Monsters' Hand Jive." That's our cue to go back on stage, to find Santa and lead him back to the North Pole.

"Isabelle!" I yell. "Come on! It's our cue. They're already singing 'Merry Monsters' Hand Jive.'"

Chapter 22

ISABELLE DARTS THROUGH the glowing fog. Then we both swoop back to the fire escape.

I kick away the stone and yank the door open.

Isabelle grins and her giant ears wobble as she flashes by and bounds for the stage.

"Girls! Where have you been? I couldn't find you anywhere." Mrs. Honey is frantic. "Hurry! You're supposed to be on stage right *now*."

No time to explain. We lurch up the stage steps.

Mr. Grady has launched again into our entrance cue music.

We burst on stage together.

I glance at the hushed audience. Everyone's staring. Waiting.

I gulp down fear and take a good deep breath. Then I boom out in my loudest voice:

"Oh Santa! Dear Santa,
so there you are!
We've searched and we've searched
behind each tiny star . . ."

I sing and sing while Isabelle again does some cool hip-hop moves with Santa/Mojo. She leads him across the stage and around the snowbanks. And finally to the Christmas tree at the North Pole. Just in time for Christmas Eve.

The whole cast of various monsters files on stage singing, "We wish you a merry Christmas" and ending with a loud "and a *monstrous* New Year."

The audience cheers and claps.

Isabelle holds up her hands and the audience falls silent. She motions me forward.

I swallow hard and take another deep breath. I announce in my loudest voice, "We'd all like to say thank you for coming tonight. But just before you leave, we have one more special number. A surprise. Please follow us outside through the side doors."

With a grand flourish, Mr. Grady plays the introduction for "O Christmas Tree."

Mojo grins at me through his white beard and gives me

a thumbs-up. With a jolly, "Ho, ho, ho," he leads the way off the stage.

Isabelle and I and the rest of the cast follow him, leading the audience outside through the gym's side doors.

Singing "O Christmas Tree," the whole audience files in a grand procession around the side of the school until they see it, its outline barely visible in the thick fog. Our giant Christmas tree!

"Oh, how lovely are thy branches!" I sing out, gazing up at the gorgeous sight.

The red bows glisten, and each yellow, red and green light glows in its own pale foggy halo. And the star! Not quite at the top of the tremendous tree, but certainly high enough, its lights twinkling like a real guiding star in the dark sky. Perfect.

Mr. Grady has left his piano. He makes his way to the front of the cast. Then he leads the students and the whole audience in singing "O Christmas Tree" again as we gaze up at the lovely sight.

In the front row, Mom and Dad are standing arm in arm watching me. Their eyes shine with pride.

My voice soars up and up through the swirling fog. Into the swaying branches. To the very heart of that *magnificent* tree.

When the song comes to an end, I hear a familiar voice. "Ladies and gentlemen. Just before you leave, we have an announcement."

It's Uncle Berny. He comes to the front of the crowd. The elderly gentleman follows him. Uncle Berny looks questioningly at the principal. She nods and smiles.

"Ladies and gentlemen," Uncle Berny continues in his deep voice. "I'd like to introduce Mr. Johnston. He wants to say a few words before you leave this evening."

The hushed crowd waits.

"A short announcement, ladies and gentlemen," says the man, whose voice is strong, despite his frail appearance. "I understand from some letters I've received, and even a petition, that we have something quite special here. The children have worked very hard to show us just how special this beautiful old cedar is. I wish to especially thank Isabelle Seconi and Jeanie Leclare for their great efforts. And I wish to announce that as long as I own this property, this tree will not be harmed in any way."

Everyone cheers and claps.

"And what's more," the gentleman continues, "it's so lovely like this, all lit up, I'll have it decorated in the same manner every Christmas! Now I wish you all peace and good will."

The crowd cheers again.

"All right!" Mojo yells, throwing his Santa hat up and into the crowd.

"What do you know?" Isabelle is grinning at me. "We did it, pal. We saved our tree. I can't believe we did it. Our tree is saved!"

Grinning back at her, I give my friend a high five. Then I give one to Mojo as well.

"All for one and one for all!" we all yell. "Tree Musketeers!"

As the crowd starts to break up and leave, a tall woman with red hair bustles over to Isabelle. "Oh, Issie," she says. "That was wonderful. Simply wonderful!" And she crushes Isabelle in a big hug.

"Mom, this is Jeanie." Isabelle's voice is muffled. She shakes loose and pulls me over to meet her mother. "The girl I was telling you about. My new friend."

"Jeanie. You're a real lifesaver," Isabelle's mother says, squeezing my shoulder. "You did a terrific job filling in for Isabelle up there on stage tonight."

Mom and Dad appear at my side. "We agree," Mom says, wrapping her arms around me in a hug. "We're so proud of you."

"Thanks, Mom. Here's Isabelle, my new friend, and her mother."

"Great meeting you both." Isabelle's mother shakes their hands. "I'm having a few people over for cookies and hot toddies this evening. Would you like to join us? And Jeanie as well, of course."

Mom glances at Dad, who grins and nods.

"We'd love to," he says. "Thank you."

Before Isabelle's mom can give us her address, Uncle Berny appears. "There you two are," he says in his booming voice. He pats Isabelle's head, then he picks me up and twirls me around. "The stars of the show!"

I'm a bit dizzy when he puts me down.

"Oh, you must be the Uncle Berny Isabelle told me about," Isabelle's mom says. "Now you must join us for our little party tonight as well. I won't take no for an answer."

"A party? Count me in," Uncle Berny says, winking at me. "Count me in."

"Thank you, Uncle," I whisper, grinning at him.

"And thanks, old tree." The long graceful branches of our tree are swaying gently in the evening breeze. "Thanks for finding me some new friends."

Maybe living on the coast isn't going to be so bad after all.

ABOUT THE AUTHOR

Norma Charles is the author of many books for children. Her latest book, *Runner: Harry Jerome, World's Fastest Man*, was shortlisted for the Sheila A. Egoff Prize for Children's Literature. Norma is a former teacher/librarian and enjoys visiting schools and libraries to meet young readers. She travels widely and lives in Vancouver in a home surrounded by former Christmas trees, several of which have grown taller than the house, and includes one old, magnificent cedar. Visit her online at www.normacharles.ca.